Chris
Johns

Pacific
BEACH
Hot Gay Erotica

WARNING

This book contains sexually explicit scenes and adult language. It may be considered offensive to some readers. This book is for sale to adults ONLY.

* * * * * * * * * * * * * * * * * * *

Please store your files wisely where they cannot be accessed by underage readers.

Please feel free to send me an email. Just know that these emails are filtered by my publisher. Good news is always welcome.

Chris Johns - chris_johns@awesomeauthors.org

You might also want to check my blog for Updates and interesting info. http://chris-johns.awesomeauthors.org/

About the Publisher

4Fun Publishing, a member of **BLVNP Incorporated**, 340 S. Lemon #6200, Walnut CA 91789, info@blvnp.com / legal@blvnp.com

NOTE: Due to the highly emotional reaction of some people to works of erotic fiction, any email sent to the above address that contains foul language or religious references is automatically deleted by our anti-spam software and will not be seen. All other communications are welcome.

DISCLAIMER

Please don't be stupid and kill yourself. This book is a work of FICTION. Do not try any new sexual practice that you find in this book. It is fiction and not to be confused with reality. Neither the author nor the publisher or its associates assume any responsibility for any loss, injury, death or legal consequences resulting from acting on the contents in this book. Every character in this book is over 18 years of age. The author's opinions are not to be construed as the opinions of the publisher. The material in this book is for entertainment purposes ONLY. Enjoy.

PACIFIC BEACH
Hot Gay Erotica

By: Chris Johns

ISBN: 978-1-62761-946-2

Chapter One

"You are new in town Max so listen and learn. The line between the safe areas and ones to avoid at all costs is narrow. If you stray on the wrong side of the line you will definitely be in trouble. You probably won't lose your life, but you'll lose everything else."

Max looked at Ralph with an amused disdain.

"Really Ralph, isn't that a little dramatic, even for you?"

"I mean it Max, this can be a very nasty town if you aren't street smart. I'm so pleased you came home with me but I don't want to see you in trouble if you go out without me."

Ralph had persuaded Max to spend the midterm break with him instead of going home. They had been roommates at college and had gelled very quickly. They were both gay and had soused out each other in the first week, found out that they enjoyed sex together and indulged at every opportunity. Max was the dominant one and Ralph loved to be a bottom to Max's amazing cock. No dissent there, Max was an anal virgin but had a heap of experience as a top. His best friend at school was like Ralph, a dedicated bottom and had been taking Max's cock for more than a year before college started and they had to part. Max was a typical self-confidant surfer boy. He had been brought up on the Pacific coast a couple of hundred mile South of where they were now and was drawn to the beach like a bee round a honey pot. Ralph wasn't, he was happier with his head stuck in a book, so it was bit of opposites attract with these two.

"I know you would be bored sticking with me for the whole holiday, Max, but you can do your own thing during the day and just spend your evenings with me. Mum and dad aren't going to interfere and my room is at the far end of the house so they won't hear my screams of pleasure as you ream out my ass."

Both boys laughed at that. Ralph was almost insatiable and could have multiple orgasms while Max fucked him. The feelings were mutual since Max almost always managed at least two orgasms inside Ralph before he went soft. They didn't love each other and didn't think they ever would, they just loved being friends and fuck buddies.

Parameters were agreed and Ralph had pulled out a local map to show Max where to go and not to go. The route to the beach was straightforward but Ralph emphasized that there was a clear line on the beach over which he should not explore. Max didn't heed the warning and very soon found himself in trouble with a capital T.

Their first complete day started normally. Breakfast with the parents before they went off to work and then did a quick love in for an hour before Max was itching to get to the water. Ralph showed him the route again, emphasized the dividing line between safe and unsafe and agreed to meet for lunch.

Max just carried a towel and a butt bag, his ID, and some money was all he had in the bag. He was wearing very sexy beach shorts and a tight T Shirt. The only word to describe his look was 'hot'. He spread his towel and started walking along the beach. "Don't go past lifeguard tower 3", Max remembered as he came to it, but he continued walking.

Doesn't look very intimidating to me was his thought as he waved to the beach guard. The beach curved gently and Max was soon out of sight of tower 3. He walked for another few minutes, decided there was nothing interesting or special about this stretch of beach and turned to go back. As he turned he caught site of the house at the edge of the dunes. It was a cross between a beach hut and a proper house. It looked well cared for, but stood by itself it looked a little incongruous. Continuing his turn he was confronted by four boys, about his own age or a little older. They were a mix of colors, but to a man they were well put together and Max couldn't help noticing, well-endowed, as they were all wearing Speedos. The obvious leader of the four addressed Max.

"What are you doing here white boy?"

Max shrugged and just replied, "Exploring."

"Well we'll help you, starting with the house on the dune," pointing at the house that Max had just noticed. Max remembered then, Ralph's warning so he continued walking angling to go round the group of guys.

"Thanks, but I need to get back now." In a flash, they were on him and two of them had his arms twisted up his back, painfully, and started to march him towards the house. The leader spoke again.

"Behave yourself and we may let you go in a couple of days. Give us any trouble and you may find bits missing from your body."

The menace in that statement wasn't lost on Max and he took a long look at these four men.

One black one, the leader, showing an impressive bulge at the crotch, Max heard him to be called Eddie. He found out quite early on that Eddie sported a massive twelve inch cock when hard. Next was Merrick, who looked a bit Arabic, but who also sported a very large appendage. The third one was a white boy called Kolby, who looked the same age as Max. Revelation with him was a neat little cock, maybe six inches, seen later. Max thought he was cute, except that he was very hairy. The last one was, Max thought, mixed race. He was the oldest of the four. He was also the most impressive to look at. He had a beautiful body, a rich honey color, a killer smile and in his black Speedos he looked impressive, that impression doubled later when Max saw his cock. Not as long as Eddie, but very thick.

Max was surprised when he was inside the house. It looked well cared for and quite luxuriously furnished. Eddie then addressed him.

"You can do as you are told and leave here in one piece, or you can fuck us about and we'll damage you. When the boys release you I want you to get naked, immediately."

He nodded and Max was free. The silly boy bolted for the door, which had he been more perceptive he would have noticed had been locked as soon as they entered. As a result, he was caught and his T Shirt and shorts were ripped off him before he was held down over the back of a chair.

Zeke delivered five slaps to his arse that had Max howling, the guy had used all of his obvious strength. He was released again and Eddie spoke.

"Each time we punish you, the number of strokes you get will double, we will also replace the hand with a cane. Co-operate or be damaged, your choice."

Max wasn't stupid. The pain from five with a hand was awful, with a cane he was sure it would accelerate into the realms of terrifying, so he nodded.

"Now get down on your knees in front of Zeke. Remove his Speedos and show his cock how much you love it."

Max had no problem in principal to sucking cock since he sucked Ralph every day, doing it under duress wasn't what he wanted though! He went into sex mode and nuzzled the pouch of the speedo until the cock was too long and hard to remain covered, then he lowered the Speedos baring the longest and thickest cock he had ever seen. He sat back on his haunches and looked at in awe. It was incredible, not an ugly cock despite its size. *God, Ralph would orgasm just thinking about that in his love chute*, was Max's thought looking at it before moving his hand up to feel it along the whole of its length.

Max played with Zeke for ages, using all his skills to pleasure the body as well as the cock and balls. He couldn't take an awful lot in his mouth but he did manage to have Zeke gasping with his efforts. It was a good ten minutes before Zeke orgasmed, filling Max's mouth to overflowing with the volume of cum he jetted out.

"Fuck, Eddie, plan to keep this guy until the end of the holidays that was the best blowjob I've ever had."

Max wondered then if he had done the right thing making it so good.

"In that case you can repeat it on our baby, Slut."

Kolby stepped up then, took his Speedos off and sat in a chair with a broad grin on his face, already rock hard ready for action.

Max didn't need telling what to. He was between Kolby's legs and licking one rock hard cock in no time. It felt weird, licking a hairy ball sac and hairy thighs, but Kolby was obviously enjoying it, and nearly went into orbit when Max deep throated him, massaging his shaft with his throat. The boy's cock was a quite thick six incher with a clearly defined glans, which Max punished with his tongue. Kolby didn't last very long and Max had another mouthful of cum.

Eddie patted him on the head and pointed at Merrick.

"His turn now, Slut. For him, come up on your knees so that I can get at your other end."

That made Max gulp. He told Eddie he was anal virgin. "Please don't touch me down there."

That was a totally wasted comment, because Eddie laughed and said, "Touch you down there, we are going to fuck you raw down there."

Merrick had a great body and a slim but long circumcised cock. Max couldn't deep throat him and was distracted by Eddie starting to work on his ass. Not good. Merrick was affronted that he was getting a poor blowjob and Max paid for it.

"I'm not going to spoil the look of your ass now, we want to take pleasure from it, but you are going to get ten with the cane for that pathetic performance." Merrick had been so disgusted he had finished himself off with his own hand.

Eddie climbed onto the couch and lifted Max's legs high and wide before pushing down on the backs of his thighs until they were nearly touching his torso. Max watched in horror as Eddie's twelve inch monster edged towards his anus. He felt it touch, wiggle around a little until it was centered on his hole and then Eddie pushed forward and his glans passed over Max's sphincter causing a huge inhalation of breath. The spike of pain was grim but not unbearable. Eddie continued sliding in and Max screwed up his face in pain until Eddie stopped with about half of his monster embedded.

"Relax boy or the pain is going to get worse."

The pain eased, Max relaxed more and Eddie started fucking, penetrating a little more each time. There was another huge tranche of pain as Eddie entered his large intestine, but then it all changed. Eddie slow fucked him and the pain each time he entered Max's large intestine decreased until the overall action became incredibly erotic and his once soft cock started to elongate. Kolby was fascinated, realizing that Max had a gorgeous cock, uncut and eight or nine inches long. By choice he was passive, he wanted to feel it reaming him out. He knew Eddie would allow it so in the meantime he knelt beside Max and started playing with his cock and balls, leaning in occasionally to suck on them as well. He played with his nipples and was pleased with himself when Max had a terrific orgasm. Kolby swallowed all his cum and continued sucking gently on the glans while he continued playing with the nipples.

Eddie was into his stride now and started hitting Max's prostate every time. Kolby kept playing and was amazed when he realized Max wasn't going soft.

"Hey, look Ed, everyone, our Slut must love being fucked, he has just cum and he is still hard."

Eddie laughed so hard he orgasmed and started peeing at the same time. He couldn't see any point in stopping so he emptied his bladder completely.

"Tighten your ass, Boy I don't want you spilling any of my piss on the floor, and follow me."

Max waddled after Eddie feeling about as low as it was possible to feel. He had now sucked three strangers, been fucked by one of them and then filled up with piss. Eddie wouldn't leave him and watched as he emptied his bowels.

"You might as well shower as well so that you are completely clean for the others to fuck you."

Max was devastated as this was obviously going to carry on for some time. He wasn't wrong. Merrick and Zeke both took ages fucking him in several different positions with no foreplay, just fisting themselves to an erection, lubing up and fucking to orgasm. Kolby was last and surprised Max.

"Eddie, will you tell him he has to make love to me as good as he knows how?"

Eddie grinned.

"You heard him Slut. Kolby is our baby, I want you to make love to him like your life depended on it being exquisite for him, because it may do."

They went through to a bedroom and with Max and Kolby on the bed the others sat around in armchairs as he started. This boy was seriously cute. Making love to him wasn't going to be a problem at all, even with the others watching. The hair was not to his liking, but everything else was. Max tried to shut the others out of his mind as he attacked Kolby's body.

He had always been a tender and gentle lover with Ralph because he was small and cute, and Kolby was small and cute as well so it came natural to Max to treat him the same. It didn't take him long to get used to the soft fur on Kolby's body and soon had the boy spacing out and moaning with pleasure. Max prolonged the action as long as he could. Kolby was crying tears of frustration by the time he was entered. Max had brought the boy to the point of orgasm so many times without letting him cum that Kolby was almost screaming to be allowed to orgasm.

When Max did enter him he came almost immediately and kept on cumming as Max fucked him with long deep strokes varying the speed and angle of entry making Kolby keen with the sensuality of it. When Max powered in for the last few strokes Kolby came again and passed out. When he came to again, Max was laid alongside him. Kolby rolled onto Max, kissed him passionately and cried out.

"I love you. That was the most incredible experience of my life."

The others looked at each other with something like shock written across their faces.

"If he's that good, I might let him make love to me." Eddie said it and sounded convincing, even Kolby understood what that meant. Eddie was a 100% dedicated top, and like Max had been and he was an anal virgin.

"Well he's not fucking me, but I sure as hell intend fucking him, lots of times, to make up for the piss poor blowjob."

That was Merrick.

"I'm going to as well, Eddie, because if he is as good being fucked as he was giving me my blowjob I'm going to want to keep him here as my fuck slut until we go back to college."

That was Zeke, and Max immediately caught on and realized these were all college boys on mid-term break the same as him. Four more days of this possibly, he paled at the thought.

Kolby didn't say anything to the others concerning his own thoughts, but he did ask Max his name and kissed him gently on the lips before saying, "I'm pleased to meet you Max, I think you are an amazing lover."

Merrick was torn a little by that comment because, like the others, he looked on Kolby as their baby. He had only joined them this term as he was a freshman and they were all in their last year. He had been welcomed into the previous trio because he had saved Eddie from drowning when a boat he was in capsized on the lake near college because Eddie embarrassingly couldn't swim.

Chapter Two

Kolby and Max went off to clean up and the other three returned to the lounge to talk.

"So, how evil are we going to be now that Kolby is in love?"

"Not love Eddie, lust. He can't be in love after one fuck so I don't think we need to change anything. Perhaps we go easy on the punishment until near the end so that we can take advantage of his obvious experience. I definitely want him to make love to me, except that I'm going to be the one doing the penetrating."

The other two laughed at Zeke's comment and nodded their agreement. It looked as though Max would be taking at least three cocks and feeding his into one anus. How many times would depend on how horny the guys were.

When Max and Kolby came back in, Eddie looked at his watch and decided it was lunchtime.

"We'd better secure our love bug until after lunch."

Max hadn't noticed it before, but hanging from the beams that supported the roof were two ropes with loops on the end and a chain hoist in the center. His wrists were placed in the loops and the ropes pulled up. Because of their position on the beam the ropes spread Max's arms very wide, a spreader bar was used on his ankles so that he was now secured in a star position. He wasn't uncomfortable, but he felt embarrassed all over again as the four looked at him before setting about getting lunch. Kolby brought sandwiches to him and fed him.

He was talking to him softly and caressing his body, particularly his groin area. Max couldn't believe that this boy was being so gentle and caring.

When they we all fed and watered Kolby whispered to Max, "I won't be able to stop the guys all fucking you but I will try to stop them punishing you when the time comes for them to get rough."

Max didn't like the sound of that, just the five slaps had been very painful and he didn't want to think what ten with a cane would be like.

The boys released Max's wrists and laid him on the floor before hooking the spreader bar to the central chain and hauling it up so that his shoulders were still on the floor, but his anus was about twelve inches clear. Merrick and Zeke knelt either side of him and at a nod from Eddie, they pulled his cheeks apart as far as they could, opening up his anus for Eddie to poke around in it for a few minutes. He then took several of the large cushions off the furniture and put them under Max's lower back.

"Lower the bar Kolby until we can pull the slut a bit further forward forcing his knees down to his shoulders."

The others could see immediately what that achieved. It opened Max up even further.

"Kolby, you love this guy, take my place here and pleasure his anus and his cock and balls while I get some toys."

Kolby was torn, he wanted to play with Max because he thought he was so sexy, but he didn't want to embarrass him by doing it in front of the others. He knew he had no choice though and knelt at Max's ass and started to play. Despite the humiliation Max couldn't help but get an erection. Zeke and Merrick joined in then concentrating on Max's rectum, spreading it even wider and finger fucking him jointly. Eddie returned with a bag which he dropped by the side of Max, and he told Kolby to move. Taking his place Eddie opened the bag and pulled out a cock ring. He fastened it round Max making the comment that now he could stay hard all day. Next came a dildo that made everyone gasp.

Kolby was almost crying as he begged Eddie not to use that on Max. Max looked in horror at the monster Eddie was waving about.

"I have been keeping this in reserve, hoping that one day we would find a slut to take it. It's nine inches round and fourteen inches long. From the tips of my fingers to just below my elbow is fourteen inches, but my forearm gets to ten and a half inches round. Game plan is that he takes both before we let him go."

Merrick was almost bouncing with glee looking at the monster and at Max's ass.

"I want to go first trying it," and Eddie laughed.

"Ok Merrick, you can go for the first six inches, open him up as much as you can first though."

Eddie and Zeke sat and watched as Merrick, using lots of lubricant opened Max up getting to the last knuckle on his hand before finger fucking him with all five digits, rotating them all the time. After ten minutes he tried opening the fingers out once they were inside Max. It looked amazing and Eddie disappeared again returning with a camcorder.

"Start again Merrick, with just one finger and increase to where you are now."

Kolby was crying and stroking Max's torso, whispering calming words to him, but Max was almost fixated on watching the action at his lower regions. When he saw Merrick reaching for the gel and the dildo he started to sweat and begged them not to fuck him with the dildo.

Eddie grinned at him, "Hey, you'll be in the Guinness book of records after today. We'll measure the dildo on camera and watch it penetrating you all the way, and then do the same thing with my arm before I go in as well."

When Merrick was ready, he placed the head of the dildo at Max's anus and told him to relax. Max did the opposite and used his muscles to tighten up his anus. That didn't work because Merrick and Zeke plastered his butt with ten very hard slaps before Merrick pushed hard and got the glans over Max's sphincter. The pain made his eyes water, but Merrick had done such a good job of opening him up that it was tolerable. Everyone watched as Merrick saw Max's reaction and proceeded to bury the first six inches in Max's ass. It looked incredible. Even Kolby stopped what he was doing to watch, and Max couldn't believe he actually had the thing in his ass and was still conscious. Merrick fucked him with six inches for a few minutes, feeling the entry get easier all the time.

"Ok, Zeke, you take over. Pull it out and re-lube it then see if you can go to ten inches, then I'm going to try for the prize, unless you want to do the last four inches Kolby."

"No Eddie, please don't make him take any more."

Eddie liked Kolby, he was a great fuck on a regular basis back at college and he didn't want to lose that.

"I tell you what, Kolby. Zeke can go to ten, but if you'll sleep with me tonight and let me keep my little Eddie in you all night, fucking you whenever I get an erection, I'll leave your little slut until tomorrow, giving his anus a chance to lose some of the soreness. I'll even let you cream his insides before we go to bed."

Kolby thought of the offer as a reprieve that he could work on the next day so he agreed. Zeke did as Eddie suggested, and once again, Max's ass was the center of attention. Zeke fed it slowly until he had reached Merrick's limit and then continued, knowing he would go through the second barrier very soon. At seven inches he did, entering Max's large intestine with a huge tranche of pain that had Max gasping to control it. The last three inches were relatively pain free, and when Zeke started long stroking Max, each entry was less painful until Max started to find it erotic and got an erection. He was gutted that he could react this way to such an awful violation of his body.

The culmination of that session though was Max having an orgasm because of the punishment his prostate took from the monster. Eddie couldn't believe it and was so turned on that as Zeke pulled the monster out that Eddie went in for a very quick fuck. Zeke and Merrick followed, before they released Max and let Kolby take him to a bedroom to clean him up and pamper him.

What an act of love that turned out to be. Kolby gathered up wash cloths, towels and cream before returning to Max's bed and gently cleaning him up and creaming his bottom inside and out. When all was finished, he tucked Max in bed and sat stroking him until he fell asleep. There was no risk of him being able to escape because the windows all had security bars set on the outside. Kolby re-joined the others in the lounge and pleaded with Eddie to take it easy on Max the next day.

"He is such a nice guy Eddie, please don't abuse him anymore, and please don't tear up his ass like you normally do."

Food for thought.

"I'll think about it. You can help by being uber enthusiastic when we have sex tonight."

Kolby nodded, he loved sex and even Eddie's twelve inches had been accepted after so many fuckings during the last semester.

The next morning Kolby went into Max's room and found him quietly sobbing as he thought about what was going to happen that day.

"What is it Max, are you hurt?"

Max shook his head, "No, I'm just thinking about what I am going to have to put up with today, and I know my friend will be worried sick that I didn't come back from the beach."

Kolby thought about it and decided that if he couldn't make the other's leave Max alone, he would find some way of getting him out of the house. He reassured Max that he would do anything he could to make it ok for him.

"Go and have a shower Max and then come through to the kitchen for breakfast."

He left Max and went to see the others.

"I want you to lay off Max completely today Eddie and let him go. I'll be your sex slave today and you can do anything you like to me, but you leave Max alone. If you don't I'm never going to have sex with any of you again when we get back to college."

Eddie just laughed.

"I mean it Eddie. All three of you think about it, no sex with me ever again."

The other two looked at Eddie and Zeke spoke up.

"We only have two more days Eddie. Today we can have as much kinky sex as we want to with Kolby, so all we lose out on is tomorrow. In exchange for that we have our little sex toy for the next semester and a half until we graduate. I think I'll vote for Kolby's proposal."

"Me too," said Merrick, "We can always let Max stay and watch. If he wants to relieve some of the pressure on Kolby he can volunteer to take part on the understanding we release him at the end of the afternoon."

Eddie could see the possibilities there and agreed.

"Ok, Kolby, get naked and then go and fetch your lover."

Max was surprised to see Kolby naked and even more so when Eddie laid out the plan.

"You remain here today, Max, and witness Kolby taking what you would have taken. We will release you then at the end of the afternoon. If you elect to join Kolby to relieve the pressure on him, you can, but otherwise you just watch. You don't touch your cock however turned on you get unless you are taking part. Agreed?"

Max couldn't believe his luck and nodded enthusiastically.

"Ok Kolby, get the oversized butt plug and install it in your ass, then get our breakfasts."

Max hated watching Kolby struggle to get the thing in particularly as it went over his sphincter causing a huge chunk of pain. Once it was settled in however it started to impact his prostate as he moved around the kitchen causing him to get a hard on. It looked so sexy that Max got an erection as well making him blush.

"I'm sorry Kolby, it's just that you look so sexy with an erect cock."

"I don't mind Max, I like it that you find me sexy."

The three guys played with Kolby at every opportunity as he served breakfast, and Max was almost peeing pre-cum cause it looked so erotic. Breakfast cleared away and Zeke started.

"Lean over the breakfast bar Kolby, spread your legs as wide as you can and use your hands to pull your butt cheeks apart."

Eddie made Max stand so that he had the best view, then Merrick and he together started fingering Kolby, pulling his anus as wide as they could. When the guys had three fingers each inside Kolby and were stretching him even more, Max had his first orgasm. It was so erotic even though Max was bleeding for Kolby taking the abuse. He could see why the others indulged in this kind of sex though. It was incredibly stimulating to watch to the point where hands free orgasms were possible.

The next action made Max cry eventually as the three guys took turns power fucking Kolby, each one having at least two orgasms. He was allowed to take Kolby to his bedroom to clean him up and use a soothing cream inside his butt after that.

"We have to get out of here Kolby or they are going to damage you."

It was quite obvious Kolby was in pain and realized Max was right. He couldn't understand these three seniors. Yes, they had used him at college, pretty extensively, but never like the last hour.

"The only way we can do this is to get the door unlocked without them knowing and then make a run for it, even if we are naked."

Max agreed but not knowing the house that well he suggested he take Kolby's place with the boys for the next session and hope that he was in a fit state to run when the time came.

"Eddie, I'm taking Kolby's place for now. You have made him very sore."

"Ah, how sweet, our little sex toy wants to protect his lover."

Max could almost hear Eddie's brain working and realized he was in for some serious abuse. He followed Eddie's eyes that were now scanning the ropes hanging from the beams.

"Let's get his ankles in the rope loops."

Max could see what was going to happen and wanted to run, but nowhere to go so he lay down under the beam when instructed and watched his ankles being secured in the loops that were pulled tight. He thought running away after being held upside down in those would not be possible and he expected his ankles to be too painful. The ropes were pulled and he ascended until his hands couldn't touch the floor and his legs were spread so wide he thought he was going to be split in two. The three monsters started then. Fingers were first, increasing in numbers until Max lost count. He knew he was opened incredibly wide, but the only pain was in his ankles. He saw the dildos come out then and he spent a long time being fucked by them and played with. It was ridiculous how he kept cumming because the dildos had been well lubricated and felt incredible as they systematically pounded his prostate before entering his large intestine.

Kolby was being ignored and had no trouble reaching the door and unlocking it. He also managed to get a bundle of his clothes and set them down by the door as well.

Meanwhile, Max wondered at the sensuality of the sex he was being subjected to. If his ankles were more comfortable it would have been sensational. After about a quarter of an hour the guys pulled up a bench and lowered him until he was comfortably on his back but with his legs still wide spread. Merrick was first then to fuck him. He was stood over Max and fucked in a rotating manner making Max squeal with pleasure, he had never felt anything so sensational in his life until Merrick came planting what seemed like gallons inside him. Zeke took over then and just straight fucked him hitting his prostate every time because of the thickness of his cock. Eddie was last and hurt because he power fucked him but it didn't stop Max having another orgasm, dry at last after so many fantastic ones with Merrick and Zeke. Released from his restraints Max didn't have the strength to move for ages, letting Kolby clean him up and cream his insides which weren't particularly sore, just well used.

The guys disappeared into the kitchen then and Kolby thought it was time to make their move. They crept to the door and had time to put on clothes. Kolby was so close to Max's size that there was no problem. They opened the door quietly, exited and closed it behind them. Then they ran, angling down to hit the beach at the lifeguard station that marked the beginning of Max's nightmare. Along the beach and they were amazed to see Max's towel still in place. They picked it up and continued running, not stopping until they were at Ralph's house.

"Ah, I was right not to call the police when you didn't come home."

That comment greeted them as they entered the house.

"It didn't take you long to find a diversion."

Ralph didn't sound pissed off. He knew that Max wasn't in love with him, they were just friends who found common ground for their sexual relief.

"You don't know the half of it. This is Kolby, my savior from some pretty extreme sex. Kolby this is my friend Ralph."

Introductions complete and Max told Ralph his tale of woe. Ralph could hardly believe it but did manage an "I told you so," at the end.

"What are we going to do about the guys and our gear, Kolby?"

"Well, I will probably need to think about a new college, but I'll call them now if I can borrow a 'phone and warn them off."

The warning and instructions were pretty unequivocal.

"Eddie, I want you to pack up mine and Max's gear and Merrick, by himself, is to deliver it to me, five hundred yards beyond lifeguard tower 3 towards tower 2 in exactly one hour from now. Any interference or deviation from that and Max will go to the police. I might see you back at college, but don't count on it."

Kolby grinned at the other two.

"I don't think we'll have any trouble, none of them will want to see their degrees go down the drain having worked for so long to get them." Ralph grinned then.

One hour later Kolby was back in the house with all their gear and an assurance from Merrick that there would be no problem back at college and they were sorry they had been so beastly to both of them.

"I don't know what mum and dad are going to say when I tell them three of us will be sleeping in the same bed tonight." That was Ralph's opener after Kolby's return.

The other two looked with shock written across their faces.

"But there is a spare bedroom Ralph."

"I know, but I can't get spit roasted if Kolby is in there, and you are going to spit roast me all night aren't you?"

Kolby looked shocked and Max just curled up laughing and spluttered out a quick, "Slut," before nearly falling over.

When Ralph's parents came home and were told that the new boy was going to share their bed for their last night they didn't say a word. Max and Kolby were so surprised that Ralph's dad just laughed and said, "Just make sure you don't gang up on Kolby because he's the new boy."

No surprises that the boys disappeared to Ralph's room very quickly after dinner.

"We'd like you to join your mother and me for breakfast before you head back to college so don't stay up all night."

Max could hardly contain himself until they were in the bedroom.

"They have to know, Ralph."

Ralph grinned.

"Of course they do. I told them when I first realized I was gay and then when I realized I wanted to be a slut my dad just told me to be careful and enjoy it."

They all did that night. It started with Ralph telling Max what he wanted.

"You know what I like Max, and Kolby has all that experience with the three animals so you two can do anything you like to me as long as at some point I have one of you in each end. I know I like to suck, and I love to be fucked, particularly by your monster, Max but I'll be happy for you to change ends if you like for two spit roasts."

"Alright, Slut, first things first, we all shower, no playing until we are out here again."

After the job was done there were three boys, shiny as new pins and glowing with anticipation.

"Display, Ralph, let Kolby explore your body."

No dissent from either party. Kolby had fun for a few minutes stroking Ralph, bringing him to an erection in seconds and having him cooing with pleasure when Kolby checked out his insides with a couple of fingers, lubricated, of course. This was to be a night of unbridled, but enjoyable sex.

Ralph insisted on wearing his peaked sailor cap which looked silly as he was naked from the cap down, but it made the boys laugh. Kolby showed where his interest lay pretty quickly. He spent an age playing with Ralph's butt, it was so cute and sexy he couldn't stop stroking it and fingering it, moving close to lick the cheeks as well. He did move round occasionally to play with the very attractive cut cock that was surprisingly big.

"I think I want him to fuck me as well as the reverse, Max, he is very sexy."

"I am here you know, you can tell me."

Kolby laughed, "Sorry, Ralph, you are one very sexy guy. I think I might try to change colleges at the end of the semester if we can do this often."

More laughter was heard until Kolby took Ralph in his mouth and swabbed his glans. Ralph's sharp intake of breath was testament to the effect that Kolby's tongue had on it.

"I think we need to get our love bug on the bed, Kolby, and do some serious damage to his insides at both ends." Ralph didn't need telling twice, he was on his back, legs bent and spread before you could say Robinson Crusoe.

Max watched more than participated as Kolby made love to Ralph. It was magic and made Max monstrously hard but he didn't touch either of the other two until Kolby swung round to get between Ralph's legs, then he dangled his very hard cock over Ralph's mouth. He had to push it down hard because it was hugging his belly. He mouth fucked his mate gently watching Kolby open him up before entering him. Kolby pushed Ralph's thighs down, spreading them more as he did so until the view Max had made him orgasm, almost choking Ralph with the volume of his cum. He had never seen anything as erotic in his life. Ralph started to orgasm very quickly and didn't appear to stop until Kolby had a mighty orgasm and Max followed with his second. Kolby had so much experience as a bottom that he knew exactly what to do to give pleasure and Ralph was such an experienced top that between the two of them their skills were certain to create orgasms of tremendous power. Kolby surprised the others then by rolling forward to lick up all of Ralph's love juice, finishing by taking his cock in his mouth to clean it.

"Thank you Ralph, that was stupendous. Now will one of you

give me a good seeing too as well?"

That was hilarious, watching Ralph and Max fighting to see who could get erect again the fastest. Ralph won and surprised Max by being first and fucking Kolby.

"But you never fuck when we make love."

Ralph grinned, "Well I guess there's a first time for everything."

The average was six orgasms each by the time they called a halt. Max had taken Ralph's pretty cock in his love tunnel and thoroughly enjoyed it, the same with Kolby's. Kolby had taken Max as well and reveled in the size of it. Three very contented boys showered again and fell into bed.

The next morning at breakfast it was so obvious that these three college boys had enjoyed their night that mum and dad looked at each other with quizzical expressions and dad offered up a comment.

"I hope this doesn't herald a problem boys, love triangles can be very difficult." Three very red faces spluttered and tried to speak at once. Ralph won.

"What do you mean Dad?"

Dad laughed and said, "Look at yourselves. If you are going to get serious with each other please be careful I wouldn't want to see any of you get hurt emotionally." Ralph teared up then and went round the table to give his father a kiss.

"Thanks, Dad, I love you so much." It was three very thoughtful boys that went to pack after saying goodbye to Ralph's parents.

"If you think we could make a threesome work, I'd like to transfer to your college next semester if they will take me." Kolby looked unsure until the other two grabbed him in a three way hug and

Ralph summed it up for both him and Max.

"Max is my sex partner. We know the spark isn't there for real commitment so if you and Max fall in love that wouldn't be a problem as long as you continue to service me."

Once again Max called his friend a slut and told Kolby, "I agree, and on my side I don't think it would be difficult to fall in love with you, but I think Ralph is very sexy and I do love him as a friend."

Kolby beamed because he was already a little in love with Max and thought it wouldn't be difficult to become a lot in love with this gentle and loving partner.

Chapter Three

During the second half of the semester Max and Kolby spoke several times a week. At the end the boys knew they were in love and looking to be together. Max found out that Kolby was an orphan, but not destitute, he just didn't know how much wealth he had.

"I've talked to Ralph, Lover, and he knows I want to take you home with me for our holiday. If my parents don't accept us we'll go to Ralph's again."

"Ok, I'll pick you up at your college if you like and we can drive to your home, or to Ralph's."

Agreed, but Max wondered what kind of car Kolby had. He hoped it wasn't a rattle trap because they had a lot of mileage to cover. He spoke to his parents next.

"Hi Mum, can you go on loudspeaker so that dad can here as well."

"Yes Dear, you can go ahead now."

"Hi Dad. The reason that I want to talk to you together is twofold. I want to bring a special friend home with me for the holiday, and I want us to share my bed."

Mum jumped in the quickest.

"What do the girl's parents think about that?"

"It isn't a girl Mum, it's a boy, and I think I'm in love with him."

Dad jumped in then.

"Let's cut the innuendo Son, tell it like it is."

"Ok, Dad. I'm gay. I so want you to accept it because I love you both so much, but Kolby is an orphan and I want to be with him this holiday."

There was quite a long silence before dad came back.

"Would you like us to move the double bed from the guest room into your bedroom to give you more room in bed? Your single will be a bit tight."

Max was soon crying with relief and pleasure. Through his sobs he managed to say.

"Yes please Dad. We'll be home the day after tomorrow."

When Kolby picked him up, Max was wide eyed. Kolby was driving what looked like a brand new KIA SUV, obviously top of the range when he looked inside and saw the soft leather seats and the dashboard with its central screen.

After a very long and passionate kiss Max spoke.

"Wow Lover, that's a serious piece of kit, it must have cost a bomb."

Kolby blushed a little, "Yeah, it did take a lot of my allowance." Then he giggled and the matter was dropped.

They drove to Max's home chattering away as though they hadn't spoken for months instead of just the previous day. Max couldn't keep his hands off Kolby, stroking and touching him all the time.

"I've really missed you Babe. Are we going to have to do this again when we return to college?"

Kolby grinned.

"No. In college I will transfer and I'm still going to study the same subjects. The only condition is that my guardian set is that he says he will cut my allowance and confiscate the car if I let my grades drop. We'll have to make love at my desk so that you can fuck me while I carry out my assignments."

Two very happy boys drew up at Max's parents' house towards sunset.

"Hi Mum, hi Dad, this is Kolby."

Mr. & Mrs. Western shook hands with Kolby, not smiling but nodded a greeting.

"I don't want to embarrass you son, but your mother and I need to know what footing to put your friend on. How serious is this relationship?"

Max blushed at his father's bluntness.

"On my part it is becoming more serious every time I talk to Kolby."

Looking at Kolby dad continued, "And what about you, Son?"

Kolby stood just a little straighter and replied in a firm voice.

"I fell in love with Max the first time we met. I don't see that changing anytime soon."

"In that case Boy, I think you had better call us Mum and Dad."

That comment set the stage for the boy's holiday. It was very relaxing and full of love and laughter. Because of the car, Kolby had to let out a little of his circumstances. He held back as much as he could because he didn't want Max to know just how wealthy he really was.

The first night was, surprisingly, sex free. They were both very tired after the drive and a long after dinner talk with the parents. They fell into bed and Kolby kissed Max goodnight before turning over and spooning into him. Of course they both had erections and were sleeping naked.

"I do love you Max, and I doubt you will get the chance very often to go to sleep without making love to me, so make the most of tonight."

Max nibbled his lover's ear and whispered, "That is for sure Babe. I love you so much." They drifted off to sleep feeling as contented as it was possible to be.

Breakfast the next morning was fine because mum and dad both had to go to work, but after dinner that evening Kolby got the third degree. He managed to sidestep most of the questions relating to his financial circumstances. He just said that his guardian was quite generous provided he worked hard at college.

"I promise that by moving to Max's college I won't hurt his grades because I need good ones as well to keep my allowance." Kolby laughed off the comments about moving colleges being difficult. It wouldn't have done to say that money talks.

The Western's knew, by the end of that holiday that they had two sons now and just hoped that neither of them would ever be hurt by this relationship.

The first complete day set the tone for the holiday. Mum and dad off to work, Max grabbed Kolby and planted a passionate kiss on his lips.

"I love you Kolby, and I want to take you to bed right now to show you. I have never had the chance to properly make love to you, taking my time to show you how I truly feel."

Kolby was intrigued, Max looked so serious and spoke with such feeling. The eyes finalized Kolby's feeling that he was going to take a trip round the planets as he was taken to Paradise.

They showered with Max carefully cleaning Kolby's lower regions, he used one soaped finger to clean his anal entry and made sure he rinsed it carefully as well. The remainder of the body was treated as gently but even the monstrously hard erection didn't make Max play too long.

"When that spits next, I want it to be the most amazing orgasm you have ever had."

Kolby wondered just exactly what Max was going to do with him. He didn't have to wait long though. All washed and dried, Max led Kolby to his bed and laying down beside him started to caress his body and kiss his face, particularly his lips as he told him.

"I love you Babe, I am so pleased we are going to be together always now. I know you are going to be a long term influence on my life, and I promise I will never hurt you. I know I'll make mistakes sometimes by saying or doing the wrong thing. You must tell me so that I can correct it. I never want you to be sad that we are together."

Kolby took this all in and wondered how he could be so lucky. His uncle was the only family he had left, but affection wasn't part of the relationship. His uncle was always punctilious in his behavior when Kolby would have liked a hug or a cuddle. The three sex hounds had got the use of his body by being nice to him. Yes, he loved the sex, but if they hadn't been affectionate as well he would have forgone the pleasure of being fucked and being able to blow such gorgeous cocks. Now he had Max who showed at every opportunity that this, for him, was the real thing.

That was how the holiday went. Being able to make love as often as they wanted and being able to sleep together was heaven for both boys. They loved the sex, but they loved the companionship and emotional closeness much more. Kolby could have either orgasmed, or cried with pleasure at the cuddles and words of love heaped on him by Max.

They went off to college together at the end of the holiday, as happy as could be. Kolby left with the idea that he had new parents and a new lover. Max knowing he had found his life's soul mate, with any kind of luck.

First problem when they arrived back at college was that Kolby wasn't in Max's dorm, not even in the same block. Kolby was systematic in his approach to change that. He met Max's roommate, was very interrogative towards him finding out what he was studying, what he liked and disliked, how wealthy, or otherwise were his family. Knowledge analyzed and the next day he approached him when Max wasn't around.

"Kent, can you keep your mouth shut when required?"

"Yes Max, but what's this about?"

"Very simple. I want to share a room with Max. I would be very happy to pay you to swap with me."

Kent was a little taken aback by that.

"You don't have to pay me, student admin would do that if you put a strong enough case and Max just has to say I disrupt his routine."

"I know, but that would be underhand and not fair to you, besides, Max says you are a nice guy."

"Ok, if it's that important to you I'll move, today if you like."

Kolby shook hands with Kent and then nearly floored him.

"If you swear to say nothing to Max I'd like you to have this."

'This', turned out to be an envelope with $1,000 in it.

"Oh no Kolby, I can't take that."

"Yes you can. I want you to because it is worth ten times that to share with Max."

Kent clicked then.

"Oh gosh, you two are lovers aren't you?"

Kolby nodded and was surprised when Kent grinned at him.

"Damn, I shared with him for a semester and never thought to try to get into his pants."

Two boys were laughing happily as they packed Kent's gear and took it to his new dorm and then brought Kolby's back. What a love was shared betwee Max and Kolby had that night, even if it was in a very narrow bed. The result of that first full day was a constant foursome for the whole semester, Ralph and Kent making up the foursome. By the end of the semester it was two couples because Ralph and Kent had become lovers.

A LITTLE over three years later, four happy young men had a private graduation party where Kolby dumb founded them all. After ordering their meal at a very swish restaurant where Kolby had taken them and assured them they would not get a bill, he told them.

"When I reached 21, I took control of my inheritance. That means I own 87% of Kolby Enterprises, you may have heard of them."

Max gulped, "Do you mean, The Kolby Enterprises?"

Kolby nodded.

"Yes."

All three of the boys were almost speechless. Max was the first to speak again.

"But that makes you a multi billionaire."

Kolby nodded.

"Yes, it does. My uncle decided that when my parents died he wanted me to grow up with my feet firmly on the ground so he virtually cast me adrift. He supported me with a reasonable allowance but I had to turn in good grades and I couldn't call on any of my inheritance. The result has been that I have three friends that are better than any I could have bought because I know they are real. One of them is the man I hope I am going to grow old with. On top of that I have a new mum and dad that I love almost as much as I loved my birth ones. Now I intend to show those friends what true friendship is. I know that none of you have jobs to go to and I don't think you even know what you want to do."

Kolby laughed then and he continued.

"You are all going to take one month of first class holiday, these envelopes will make certain of that."

He gave Kent and Ralph each an envelope, that when the boys opened them contained $10,000 each.

"You don't get one Max because I guess you are stuck with me and will be using my credit cards for our month off."

Addressing them all again he continued.

"At the end of your month if you wish, you can book into the hotel, details on the paper in your envelope. You will telephone the personnel manager at Kolby and arrange an appointment. He has been instructed that each of you is to go through an advisory program on careers within our group. Basically, all four of us are going to start our careers at Kolby with equal opportunities to make it to the top. I'm lucky, if I don't make it on merit I just become life president."

The others laughed because Kolby had made it sound so funny.

The others were stunned and didn't speak again until they accepted their first course. Champagne came at the same time and Kolby proposed a toast.

"To the fabulous four of Kolby enterprises."

During the remainder of dinner the boys all discussed where they wanted to go. It looked very much as though they could all become main board VPs without treading on each other's toes.

There was much laughter that night until they said their farewells and headed for bed before going home the next day. Max was still blown away by the knowledge he had.

"I don't know how I am going to handle this Lover. Your kind of money frightens me. You know the kind of background I come from."

Kolby looked frightened.

"You aren't going to bail out on me are you just because you've found out I'm rich?"

Max was confused, the money sounded monstrous.

"I love you so much Kolby, but this is, I don't know, scary."

"It needn't be, we can ignore it and live like we would have done as new graduates. We don't even have to work at Kolby if you don't want to." Max gave him an odd look.

"I mean it Love, I'll slide everything I own into a trust and live the way you want. I'll do anything I have to, to keep you. Listen to me Max. I love you more than anything or anyone else in the world. I'll live in a tent if it makes you happy, but please don't throw me away."

Kolby was crying quite hard by this time making Max realize that he didn't really care about being fabulously wealthy, all he cared about was Kolby, he loved him for being him, rich or poor wouldn't make any difference.

"I'm not going to throw you away, I'm going to love and cherish you forever, and the four of us are going to make Kolby Enterprises one of the biggest conglomerates in the world."

Kolby's tears dried up immediately.

"Can we live in a mansion then and fly everywhere in a private jet. I really would like to buy you an Aston Martin to match mine as well." Max was laughing now.

"Steady Tiger, don't overload me yet. I may take a little time to get used to that kind of thing." Kolby was laughing as well.

"Ok, we'll live in a company apartment for now and walk to work, how does that sound?"

"I think I could handle that, and can I have my own bank account for my salary, and sometimes pay for things when we go out?"

Kolby wanted to keep the humor going so he frowned a little and replied.

"I'll have to think about that. I'm not even sure I'm going to sanction a salary. I was thinking more in line with some slave labor as you love me so much. I could improve the company profits even more that way. We could keep you naked as well so that I wouldn't even have to buy you any clothes. That way I could have a quick fuck anytime I want one without all the trouble of stripping you first." Max was grinning as he replied to that.

"Oh yes, I like that last bit. Lots of quick fucks as reward for jobs well done. I would be your most productive employee for that."

The soon forgot the humor or the reality of the future together. Max grabbed Kolby and took him back to bed. An hour later they resumed their day.

KOLBY WASN'T terribly subtle over the next month as he equipped both of them for young executive positions. Thousand dollar suits, handmade shoes, tailored shirts, silk socks and underwear.

"I'm sorry my love, I know this looks extravagant, but we need to look the part. Ralph and Kent are getting the same wardrobes. One of my assistants is with them sorting things out. They will also have a car to suit their status." Max was reeling under all this generosity and said so.

"Have you any idea what it would have been like for me at college if everybody had known who I really was? I would never have known who was a genuine friend and who was a gold digger, or just a plain old sycophath. Instead, what I got were three very special friends who I know like me for me, or in your case, love me for me. That was nearly four years of happiness instead of misery. My uncle was right and he thinks my decision to show you all how much that means to me is a correct one. You will all have to prove you are worth it, but you will have my support always."

Max knew he was going to learn to live with this wealth because he loved Kolby so much and realized that he was just being Kolby, helping his friends.

THE REUNION at a prearranged time after their month's holiday was all hugs and kisses. "Let's see our accommodation first, and then I can fill you in on tomorrow's routine before we go to dinner."

Kolby took them to a block of apartments quite close to Kolby Enterprises Headquarters. The first one they entered made the boys whistle.

"This is yours, Ralph and Kent. There are two bedrooms but you can just use one if you want to."

That made them laugh, and made it easier for Kolby to show them round. The place was definitely set up for senior visiting executives.

"Max and I are on the top floor, I'll give you two a key for the lift to go beyond the normal limit in the lift. Turn the key in the panel and press 'P'"

Max was wondering what kind of apartment they were going to have, assuming that the P stood for Penthouse.

"Settle in and then come up to our apartment and I'll tell you all what happens tomorrow."

Max could hardly believe what Kolby showed him. The penthouse, he was informed was used by the most senior executives.

"We are going to use it for now Max, because going to my main home every night could get quite tiresome and I don't want to freak you out too soon."

Max gulped, "I'm freaked already."

"Please don't be my love. You see, you'll soon get used to it."

Max thought, *'I hope so, this is luxury to the nth. degree.'*

The master bedroom was about an acre in area. Well maybe not that big, but Max knew it was bigger than the whole upper floor of his parents' home. It was magnificent, dominated by a huge bed.

"This is where we can have our orgies with Kent and Ralph."

Kolby was grinning so Max hoped he was joking.

"Would you mind very much if we did?"

Then Max knew that he wasn't.

"Let's sit down and talk about this can we?"

Kolby looked a little apprehensive now wondering if he had gone beyond acceptable limits with this man that he loved.

"I know Ralph and I were fuck buddies before I met you so I guess he wouldn't mind sex with us. I have never even seen Kent naked and as far as I know those two are monogamous the same as you and I have been for nearly four years. Do you really think we could have foursomes without damaging either relationship?"

Kolby relaxed now because the tone of Max's voice was interrogative and not condemning.

"I don't know, I just thought that because we are such good friends a romp together might be fun and exciting because both of them are sexy as all get out."

Max grinned then. "Well, I can tell you, Ralph is a good fuck because he never appears to be able to get enough cock, but I have no idea about Kent. Want to find out?" A very relaxed discussion took place then until the boys rang the doorbell.

Suitably impressed after the grand tour, Kolby sat them down and explained what was going to happen in the morning.

"We can all go in together. I'll be leaving you three in the care of a senior personnel manager who will interrogate you individually to find out what you would like to do and how you can fit into the company. If nothing suits you he will do everything in his power to place you with another company in the area. I will be joining my uncle to start the process of assuming my proper role in this organization. I suggest you start as you intend to carry on so three piece suits collar and tie. Be ready to leave at 0900, easy start your first day. Lunch will be in the executive dining room with me and to give you a chance to meet my uncle. In the afternoon you'll be shown round the place and given your work station. Tomorrow evening I know uncle will want us to dine with him at the house. His house that is. He'll send a limo for us and it will be a black tie do."

Kolby gave that time to sink in while he produced a bottle of champagne.

"I know it's a little early to start drinking, but this is to welcome you officially to Kolby Enterprises with my best wishes and hope that you will still be here to collect your retirement package." They all laughed at that.

Early dinner and early to bed that night so that they would all be on top of their game the next morning. Because all three boys had good general degrees they were easily fitted into departments where they showed an interest. By lunch time they knew what their career paths could be if they measured up. The personnel manager had sat them down after their interviews and laid it out for them.

"Mr. Matthews, that's Kolby's uncle has left this directive concerning you three. You are to be given every incentive to advance within this organization. However, he will not tolerate lame ducks, so you are on a fast track but you have to prove you are worth it. Being Kolby's friends gets you the opportunity but no special privileges. Well, not quite. You are all to have your own offices, which is not normal for new graduates. Just make sure you don't let Kolby down. We all think he is a very special young man."

Max felt he had to be the spokesman for them.

"Thank you Sir, we are all determined to grasp this opportunity with both hands and failing Kolby is not in our thinking."

"You will do well to call everyone Sir, until told otherwise, Max, and that starts with me. All of you please come to me if you have any queries or problems and from now on I'm Jonathon. Now, let me take you through to the executive dining room for lunch."

They were led into a room that mirrored everything else they had come to expect. Very luxurious with a large sitting area as well which is where they found Kolby, talking to a very distinguished looking gentleman. Both stood up as the boys approached.

"Hi guys, I'd like you to meet my uncle Kieron. Uncle this is Max, Ralph and Kent." Handshakes were exchanged and the boys promptly ignored the Kieron and called him Sir. Definitely the correct thing to do.

Lunch was special but they were informed they wouldn't be eating here in future.

"I'm afraid us juniors will eat in the staff canteen in future, Guys." Kieron smiled at his nephews comment.

"Well, you might get the occasional invite here so that you can all tell me how you think you are getting along. This is also a much more relaxed place for me to terminate your employment if you don't measure up." The last was said with a broad grin on his face so the boys didn't wet their knickers.

Offices were inspected after lunch and new laptops were supplied as a company welcome present, already loaded with the data that they would need to read before getting going. Three hours of reading was spent before Kolby came to collect them.

"Early finish today guys, make the most of it. You'll work hard for your salaries I promise you. By the way, happy with your employment package?"

Of course they were. Despite being told they would get no special privileges, their salaries were all above scale.

"Uncle has agreed that you two can remain in your apartment rent free for one year. That should be long enough to decide whether you are going to stay, and give you a chance to save a deposit for your own place." It was a surprise for three of them when Kent burst into tears.

"I can't believe how good you are being to me, Kolby and how much I love all you guys."

Ralph cuddled him, and Kolby smiled because he knew what none of the others did. Kent came from a family that was definitely at the bottom end of the wealth table. He had made it to college on a 100% scholarship because he was seriously clever. Of the four of them Kolby was sure he would end up the most senior in the company on merit.

One month on and the newness had worn off. They were all getting used to the luxury of their existence and making new friends. No one appeared to mind that they were open about their sexuality. Not surprising considering who Kolby was. Weekly reports on the three went to Kieron's office and were seen and discussed with Kolby.

"I think you made a good commercial choice of your friends as well as an emotional one."

Kolby was so pleased with that comment.

"We will need to keep a very close eye on Kent, Kolby or he will have my job before he is thirty."

Both had seen the department head's comments on Kent's work. As expected he was a demon.

"That won't cause any problems between the four of you will it?"

"Oh no Uncle, we will all praise him and be pleased for him."

Kieron was so proud of his nephew. Life had not been made easy for him just because his parents had been killed while he was still quite young. He had been proved right, keeping his feet on the ground with limited access to his wealth.

Kolby thought it was time now for him and Max to start expanding their sex life. He wanted it to be with Ralph and Kent, but Kent was still an unknown quantity. The only way to find out was to instigate an activity that would achieve his end without upsetting anyone. The obvious and not very subtle one would be an evening together where Kolby could suggest playing cards. One more step then to turn it to strip poker, because he wouldn't want them to get into a gambling habit that might end up costing them more than they wanted to lose.

Chapter Four

Kolby didn't even discuss his plan with Max, he thought it ought to sound natural and not something he had discussed with anyone else. They didn't all always leave work together, but one day when it happened Kolby asked the others if they would like a casual night in and he would order pizzas.

"We can just slum it for an evening and watch a movie or play cards or something. I'll order in pizzas and we have plenty of wine and beer in the apartment."

Everyone agreed and the time was set. They would all shower and change into casual wear and congregate in the penthouse at seven. First part of the plan was set and Kolby suggested they just wear sweats to be ultra-casual. Hopefully that would have them all with exactly the same amount of clothing on.

This plan worked perfectly. They sat around drinking and talking shop until the pizzas arrived. When they were all finished, Kolby went through the motions of looking for a good film to watch.

"Nothing very thrilling their guys. Fancy playing cards, or something?" It was too easy steering it to cards and agreeing on poker because that was all any of them knew.

"I don't think we should play for money that could get awkward if someone was a big loser. Why don't we play strip poker, which could be fun?" Max was very good without knowing it.

"That won't last long, none of us has much in the way of clothing to take off."

"Ok, why don't we play for forfeits and we can buy chips for articles of clothing." None of them knew how that would work, and Kolby was so pleased he had been in a clique that did this at high school.

"Ok. We start off with 100 chips each and we can bet like we would with real money. Every time you need more chips you can buy them in fifties for an article of clothing from whoever is willing to part with theirs. When you have no more clothes to buy chips with, you buy them with a forfeit. At the end of the game the guy's owed forfeits claim them. You have to end with 100 chips so extra forfeits will probably accrue at the end. We have to agree that forfeits can be anything and that means we may have to relinquish monogamy for the evening. Anyone have a problem with that?"

Kolby was looking for reaction from Kent and was surprised to see a broad grin. Three nodding heads set the tone and Kolby went to get the gaming chips. A card table was set up in the study. Kolby already knew that there was wet light in a drawer of the desk and the game began.

Kent was a canny player and soon started to show winnings as everyone else lost. This wasn't what Kolby wanted but he did manage one big win in the first session which put him in a good position at their first break to collect some clothes from Max and Ralph, as did Kent.

Articles couldn't be bought back so as fortunes ebbed and flowed they all gradually lost clothing. The winner of each exchange was allowed to remove the article of clothing from the loser and by unspoken agreement briefs or boxers were left until last. It wasn't particularly late by the time only Kolby and Kent had any articles left. Max and Ralph already owed several forfeits.

"Ok, I think we should continue until we are all naked before starting on the forfeits."

Everyone was happy with that and it was ten o'clock when Kent at last lost his briefs, not having given away one forfeit. Best laid plans came to Kolby's mind, but it would be interesting to see how Kent handled his mass of forfeits. Chips were sorted and the tally was that Max and Ralph both owed Kolby two forfeits. Max owed Kent three and Ralph owed his lover two. Kolby owed Kent one. Kent was grinning as he sat back in his chair, not making any attempt to hide his crown jewels.

"So, we never made any order about forfeits. Does that mean there are no limits and I can ask for whatever I want?" Kolby looked round saw no problem and said, "Yes as long as it takes place in this apartment."

"Oh good, in that case as Max owes me the most forfeits he can start by getting me hard and giving me a blowjob."

Max was delighted by the time he had a hard cock to look at. Kent was sporting about seven inches of uncut cock, very straight with a nice ball sac below. Max was also surprised at how buffed he was. He wasn't that good when they were roommates.

"Wow Bud, you've been working out. That body is sexy as all get out."

Kent grinned and told them. "Ralph got me into the gym because he wanted me to look as good as you Max."

Max didn't think he looked anywhere near as good as Kent but just got stuck back in giving him a very enthusiastic blow job. The balls felt good in his hands and even better when he had them in his mouth. The nipples were very sensitive little things that Max loved tweaking, just to hear Kent gasp.

Kolby was getting seriously turned on watching so he moved his chair round to continue watching while he got Ralph to blow him. He quickly realized how Max had got so good if he had been blown by Ralph very often before they met. After Ralph had brought Kolby to orgasm Kent felt wicked.

"Ralph and Max haven't orgasmed yet so I want them to use one of my forfeits each, and Ralph, I want you to fuck Max, making sure that you both cum."

Watching Ralph in action, Kolby realised he had the cutest arse of all of them. *I'm going to have my cock in that tonight* was Kolby's thought. He had seen Max fucked when they first met but this was much more fun because it was being done for pleasure by both of them. It was lovely to walk round and see it from all angles. Max was sporting his monster in fully erect mode and was obviously enjoying being screwed.

"I think you may have to do this more often Lover. I had forgotten how good it is having a cock in my arse."

Kolby laughed as he replied. "Looking at this action I think I might oblige."

Watching Max receiving Ralph's cock with so much pleasure had Kent erect again in no time.

"I may never get the chance again Kolby so I'm going for broke. I want you lying on your desk, legs well spread while I see how long I can stay in your arse before I cum."

Kent wasn't as long or as thick as Max, but it was certainly a very pretty cock and Kent was well built so Kolby expected a very exciting and sensuous screw. With Kolby in position, Kent pulled up a chair and started some serious arse play. He used his hands to spread Kolby's arse wider and dived in with his tongue. He licked and stabbed for a while before covering the anus with his mouth and sucking. Kolby nearly took off and screamed with pleasure as Kent reversed it and blew into the hole.

"Oh fuck, Kent that is incredible. Max, watch, I want this every night before you fuck me."

Max still had Ralph inside him but the two of them shuffled round to get a good view, Max now standing with Ralph hammering his prostate.

Kent started on the fingers then using his free hand to spank Kolby, very gently, but setting up a tingle that combined with the fingers had Kolby almost bouncing off the desk. Ralph orgasmed then and pulled out leaving Max free, so he went round to Kolby's head and got him sucking.

"This isn't a forfeit Lover, I just hate to see a hole unattended."

Kolby couldn't have been happier. Nothing better in the world than a cock in each end. Kent was finding it increasingly difficult not to cum because Ralph was stroking his butt and playing with his anus.

"Oh fuck, Kolby, I'm cumming." And with that he leant back and everyone could see as he powered in for his last few strokes. It looked so erotic that Max filled Kolby's throat and Kolby came in a no touch orgasm. Kent flopped back into his chair, Kolby and Max did the same and Ralph walked round looking at all the soft cocks, before wandering off to find wash the clothes and towels to clean everybody.

"If Ralph can get me hard again I want to fuck Max while Ralph gives him another blowjob then that will be me finished."

"And if I can get hard again I want to fuck Max for all of you to watch."

Max was laid on the desk cross wise on his back so that his head hung over the side and his arse over the other side. Kent pushed his thighs down when they were well spread and entered him with no preamble. Max was in heaven as Ralph climbed onto the desk to give him a blowjob at the same time, and Kolby wasn't going to be left out so he buried his cock in Max's mouth. That was actually the finale because everyone was wasted after that.

"Without doubt, that is the best orgy I have ever been involved in. I love you guys."

There wasn't much more to be said after that. Another drink for a night cap and Ralph and Kent kissed their friends good night before going down to their own apartment.

"The only thing missing from that Lover was neither of us got to fuck Kent."

Max creased up, "I know but it was fun and he does have a gorgeous cock." Just then there was a knock at the door. It had to be one of the boys so they both answered it out of curiosity. It was Kent.

"I've just realized that you two didn't get the chance to ream out my arse tonight. Not fair, so if you are ok with it I'll be back tomorrow night just to let you two give me a good seeing to." Then he was gone and Kolby and Max could only look at each other before laughing fit to bust. That was how group sex should be was the consensus as they fell into bed.

The boys were all full of fun the next day and reconvened in Kolby and Max's apartment the next night after dinner. To Ralph's delight he was able to sit and watch Kent spit roasted twice as Kolby and Max got a fuck and a blowjob each. After they all cleaned up after the action, Kent was grinning like an idiot spoke to the others.

"Now that we have all enjoyed each other's bodies we don't have to try any subterfuges to have sex. I reckon we can have orgies on request and each of us can take turns in choreographing them." The others all looked at each other before Kolby, acting as spokesman like he usually did reply.

"I think that is an excellent idea provided Max agrees for me, and Ralph agrees for you Kent. Know that a sex hound I may be, but breaking up our two partnerships isn't a possibility so 100% agreement or it doesn't happen."

"I'm ok with it Lover." That came from Max.

"I am too." Came from Ralph.

ONE YEAR after graduation, Kolby had bitten the bullet and taken Max out to the mansion that he hoped would become their main home. The house was sat on a 10 acre plot. The house itself was 16,000 square feet of unadulterated luxury. The style was traditional but the inside had been totally modernised at a cost of millions and was breathtaking. Outside close to the house was a huge swimming pool with the most beautiful pool furniture and a wet and dry bar that Max absolutely adored. A little further from the house was a sports complex consisting of squash court, two tennis courts and a gym. Further away was a stable complex with half a dozen fine horses and a fulltime stable staff to look after them.

The majority of the remainder of the land had been landscaped or tailored to look natural but tidied to make sure it was safe for riding. There was an orchard and a market garden so that much of the house food was home grown. Max found out later that they also had a smallholding that bred first class stock to feed the house with meat. The six car garage with staff accommodation above contained their cars. A Land Rover Defender for driving round the estate. Each guys matching Aston Martin's, a Cadillac SUV and a people carrier. The last bay contained a Rolls Royce Phantom that was used only for formal occasions.

The first time Max was shown round it took his breath away. Initially they just stayed in it at weekends until Max realized he was used to it and they moved in permanently. The town apartment that had afforded them so much fun was kept for nights when they were too tired to drive home or they had been to a do in town.

Max could never have dreamt of this kind of luxury and it all came about because he thought Ralph was being overly dramatic that first visit he made.

They counted their anniversary from the day Max had first slid his cock into Kolby's welcoming arse in the house on the beach. Always a source of much hilarity, shared for years with Kent and Ralph if not with the remainder of their friends and colleagues.

The boys were well into their thirties before they stopped the orgies and became monogamous. In that time Kent and Ralph had progressed on merit into senior management and bought a beautiful home only about a mile from Kolby and Max's.

Kolby's uncle died at a time appropriate for Kolby to take over the company as President and CEO. A year later, Kent took the CEOs job with two of his senior VPs being Max and Ralph.

The End

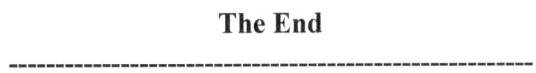

Here is a sample from another story you may enjoy:

CHRIS JOHNS

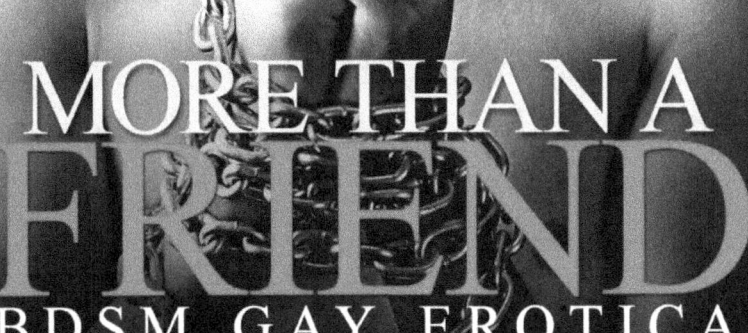

MORE THAN A
FRIEND
BDSM GAY EROTICA

Might as well do as I'm asked. I need a shower anyway, was the thought that ran through Matt's head as he sniffed his armpits.

Fifteen minutes later Alexander was back.

"Come with me," was all he said.

"But I have no clothes."

"You won't need them."

"But—"

"No buts, boy; do as you are told and come with me."

Feeling extremely embarrassed, Matt did as he was told. He had to find out what was going on, and the only way he could think to do that was to talk to the man by the pool.

Matt was nineteen and guessed the man on the sun bed to be about ten years older. As he approached, keeping a little behind Alexander, Matt noted the man, as he stood up, was probably an inch or two taller than him, well put together, without being over muscled. He couldn't see the eyes, which were covered with a pair of designer sun glasses, but noted the mid brown hair and the aquiline features, the golden tan with a dusting of hair on the chest, and, finally, the very pronounced bulge in his Speedos. He wasn't quite sure why his brain noted that fact particularly; men had never held his interest; women hadn't either, but he thought that being spaced out on drugs so often had put his sexual desires to sleep.

He stopped in front of the man and started to speak, but the man put a finger to his lips and stood in front of him.

"Listen, Matt, and learn. You will speak when spoken to, and you will obey every order given to you by me or my staff."

Matt interrupted, "Who the fuck are you?"

It was definitely the wrong thing to say. The man nodded, and before Matt could react, Alexander had him bent over a poolside table and delivered ten very hard slaps with his hand to Matt's bare arse.

Alexander was probably about six feet six inches tall, and around 225 pounds of what looked like solid muscle. A spanking from those hands was not something to want twice. Matt was howling when he was again stood facing the man, tears streaming down his face.

"As I was saying, you will call me Master at all times, and Alexander you will address as Sir. If you wish to speak, other than to answer a question, you will ask, 'Permission to speak, Master, or Sir', and wait to be given permission before continuing. If you utter any more profanities, you will be punished. Do you understand those instructions?"

Matt felt resentful, and made his second mistake.

"Yes," he mumbled.

Alexander was on him in a flash, delivering another very hard swat to his already very red ass. Matt yelped and jumped forward, almost knocking the Master over.

"Yes, what, Matt?" The man barked out.

"Yes, Master," was the now much more precise reply.

"Good. Now then, we are going to start cleaning you up before trying to turn you back into a civilised human being, inside as well. When I am finished, you will go with Alex. All of those disgusting bits of metal on you will be removed, and you will be given a respectable haircut. Then you can rejoin me for lunch. Tomorrow, you will be taken to a hospital for plastic surgery to restore your ear lobes to their proper shape. The following day, you will undergo laser treatment to remove all those tattoos, and then we will be left with a human being on the outside, instead of some painted and pierced animal. We will then spend however long we have to, training you to return to society as a useful and civilized person. Do you understand?"

Matt was fuming! "You can't do that! Let me go! You have no right to do this!" He was almost beside himself with anger, but not for long. Alexander was on him again and delivered another ten very hard slaps to a pair of cheeks already showing bruising from the first ten. Stood in front of the Master again, Matt was informed that there would be no more bare hand spankings.

"If you need chastising again, Matt, it will be with a cane. Do you understand?"

Through his sobs, Matt replied with a shaking voice, "Yes, Master."

If you enjoyed this sample then look for **More Than a Friend.**

Also by this Author:

Brotherly Love

Underworld

Revenge of the Jocks

Indian Abduction

Pleasurable Abduction

Lost

A Grip in Deep

Bullet Holes

Gay Porn Star

Delightfully Yours

Embracing the Greener Side

Promotional Desire

Aviator's Hidden Turbulence

Almost Paradise

The Hardcore Remedy

Relish Pretender

Doctor Boner

Captivated Attractions

Academically Horny

Flight of the Hornies

From the Author

If you want any more info about me, please feel free to ask! I'm a very open person so you won't offend me if you want to get more personal.

If you'd like to give me comments or suggestions to any of my books, feel free to shoot me an email at chris_johns@awesomeauthors.org.

Check my page on Amazon and my blog for Updates and interesting info.

Author Central – http://amzn.to/185Sar5
Author Blog - http://chris-johns.awesomeauthors.org/

If you enjoyed any of my books then please share the love and click like on my books in Amazon.

If you write me a review and send me an email I will send you a free book, or many.
(Just know that these emails are filtered by my publisher.)

Good news is always welcome.

One Last Thing, For Kindle Readers...

When you turn the page, Kindle will give you the opportunity to rate this book and share your thoughts on Facebook and Twitter. If you enjoyed my writings, would you please take a few seconds to let your friends know about it? Because... when they enjoy they will be grateful to you and so will I.

Thank You!

Chris Johns
chris_johns@awesomeauthors.org

About the Author

The author has drawn from his lifetime experiences as a Marine Engineer and Helicopter Pilot to take his readers round the world with his erotic stories.

Born in a small town in middle England he joined the Royal Navy straight from school and spent four years at engineering college before going to sea. After promotion to first engineer he took a career turn and trained as a helicopter pilot. The move afforded him huge opportunity to travel both as a Naval Pilot and later as a Commercial Helicopter Pilot. His Bio Pic was taken when he was relaxing in his company's social club, serving his fellow pilots and engineers with some excellent English Ale.

Retired now in the Caribbean he took up writing to compliment his other great love, sailing.

www.ingramcontent.com/pod-product-compliance
Lightning Source LLC
Chambersburg PA
CBHW060058150626
46556CB00017BA/2072